A *foreword* by the Author

"The beautiful Scheherazade's royal husband threatens to kill her, so each night she diverts him by weaving wonderful tales of fantastic adventure, leaving each story unfinished so that he spares her life to hear the ending on the morrow."

Meanwhile, the patrons of The Traveller's Joy may drink as long as they please into the wee hours, but only so long as Bacchus stays awake. So they attempt to hold his attention by spinning compelling yarns.

I fell in love with the short story while working on *Doing the Islands with Bacchus*, the third volume in this series of ten. I mean of course, the idea of the short story, (not just the shortness of it), that particular 'vivid conciseness', the 'conscious art' of Poe, which concentrates on a 'single direct effect'. Furthermore, in creating my own version of Scheherazade's 1001 nights formula, I looked forward to taking a crack at many different classic types of short story that I would not normally find myself working upon, for instance: the beast fable, the Irish blarney, the urban legend and to gratifying my illustrator's enthusiasm with references to stories by great masters like O. Henry and Dostoyevsky.

In creating these stories and in keeping with the principle that each is narrated by a different character, I wanted to give each story a distinctive voice. To achieve this effect, I sought new assistance for each piece.

The first story has art by Dylan Horrocks, the New Zealander who has long since gone on to greater things, most recently his graphic novel, *Hicksville*. Steve Stamatiadis fashioned a few effects on the next story. He was starting to investigate computers at the time and with John Passfield now runs a video games company with a staff of animators and designers.

My old pal, Wes Kublick, helped write three, including the one where I utilised his ancient Lit. expertise and we recast Gilgamesh as a Scottish soccer hooligan. Some say we should have stopped there but when I came to illustrate it, the stylistic device which suggested itself is best described as a 'cubist ransom note'. Some say we should have been drinking less but these are pub tales after all.

The next novelty was a story told without words which Marcus Moore worked up for me. Once I had this 'silent movie' in my mitts, it seemed only logical to cast Laurel and Hardy as the actors. The story of the 'bad pint' was entirely the doing of Moore. God knows, I've been away from Britain long enough to stop thinking in terms of that measure. I attempted to illustrate it in a manner that would involve the least work. We must have been running very late that month. Some of my improvised vignettes still seem funny enough. Moore was so good at this versification that I commissioned him to do the beast fable a month later.

Daren White, Moore's confrere at Dee Vee Press, offered me a script that was so neatly typed that I cut out the lines and glued them down. I usually dicker about with phrases when I buy a script but the voice in this one had an integrity that could only be damaged by tampering. I even knowingly left in a couple of typos. The same applies broadly speaking to White's version of the hospital bed legend.

In England, in 1998, I saw my brother, Mark, a down-at-heel writer/comic actor. I bought the adaptation rights to two short stories he had crammed in his breast pocket and my wife bought him three pairs of socks. I could only envision the acrobat as a Pete Mullins drawing so I called him around for a few sessions on it. The eagle-eyed may notice that I was trying to work out a lettering style for *The Spirit* story we subsequently did.

The Superguy story was me venting my satirical spleen after writing a few months of a superhero series for one of the companies. In the original, after defeating the army, I had the victorious superheroes celebrating with champagne glasses in their hands. The word came down from the editorial prohibitionists: "Lose the glasses!". Nobody seemed to notice that Big Mom was still tipsy for the first ten pages so it was inevitable that Superguy's downfall would have to involve booze.

In this way do stories come together.

Eddie Campbell, May 2000.

1001 Nights of Bacchus - Intro - page 1 - (9.90)

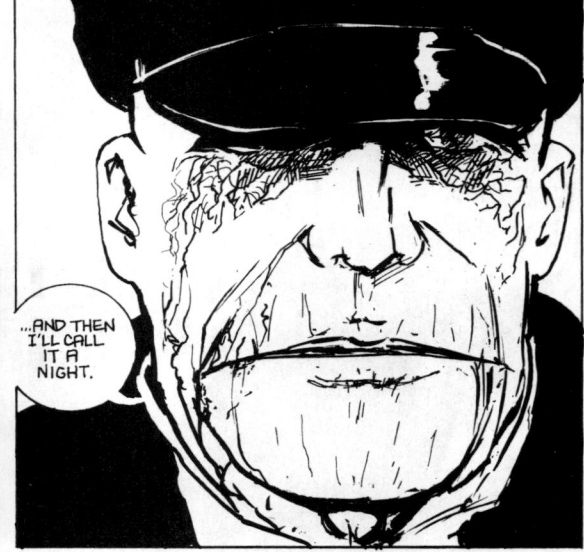

There are as many kinds of drunk as there are drinks. Here are a few. The Catholic Humility Drunk. He gets merry on a Friday night and gives his kids anything they ask for.
"What I need is a *car*, Dad."

He gets up early next morning to mow the lawn as a form of penance.

Here's the Put-Upon Drunk. Everyone's putting it upon him, grinding him down.

As he lurches off to the toilet he knocks a drink out of someone's hand, and as he throws up in the urinal he splashes it all over someone's shoes.

Here's the Talking Drunk. After two pints of brew he remembers every word he's ever read in his life.

He says some interesting things, if your brain can keep up with him at 99 r.p.m.

Here's the drunk who, as comedian Billy Connolly says, nips out for some refreshment...

And wakes up in the gutter two days later, feeling fully refreshed.

Only he can't remember what happened between these two pictures.

Henry is one of this last category. I'll tell you his story in a minute. Uh... make those doubles...and one for yourself, Hector.

Henry frets about this riddle till two days after the big race, when he pulls yesterday's unread paper out of his pocket to try to glean some clue as to what's happened during his latest absence.	He tries to wipe a dark stain off the sports page. *Is that blood?* 	As it happens, Red Rum makes the front page, and with the discoordinated faculties that normally follow a two-day bender, Henry just reads it backwards in the mirror before he thinks of turning it round. *MURDER!* 
Now to you or me it would be just an amusing little conundrum and that would be the end of it, but not to Henry. 	Here we have a man who doesn't know what he did yesterday or the day before, and his imagination is stimulated by this disturbing serendipity. 	What did he do, sleep under a bush for 48 hours? 
Or did he fly to PARIS just to say he's been in another country? 	Or did he squeeze a pretty neck with all the effort normally reserved for opening jam-jars? 	

THE MAN WHO COULDN'T SAY BOO.

COUNTING THE TILES ON THE FLOOR, HE MADE CERTAIN THAT THE TABLE WAS SQUARE TO THE WALLS AND CENTRAL IN THE ROOM.

HE SET THE TABLE WITH GEOMETRIC PRECISION, LAYING EACH PLACE EQUIDISTANT FROM THE ENDS OF THE TABLE.

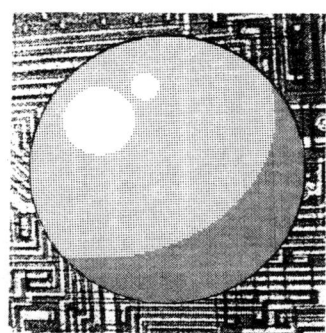

HE PLACED THE FLOWERS SO THAT THEY WOULD RECEIVE EXACTLY THE CORRECT AMOUNT OF LIGHT ACCORDING TO SUBTLE PHOTOSYNTHETIC PRINCIPLES.

HE MEASURED THE CANDLES SO THAT ONE WOULD NOT HAVE AN UNFAIR ADVANTAGE.

IT WAS HIS WIFE'S BIRTHDAY AND HE HAD PREPARED A SURPRISE.

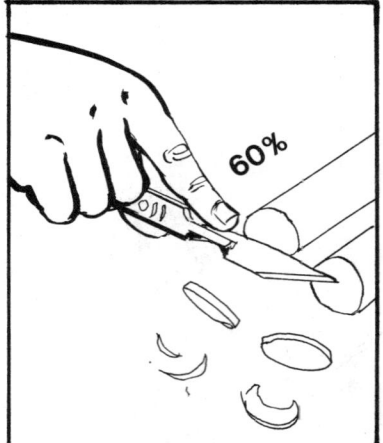

BUT WHEN HE JUMPED OUT ...

HE COMPLETELY FORGOT WHAT IT IS YOU'RE SUPPOSED TO SAY...

WHEN YOU SURPRISE SOMEONE,

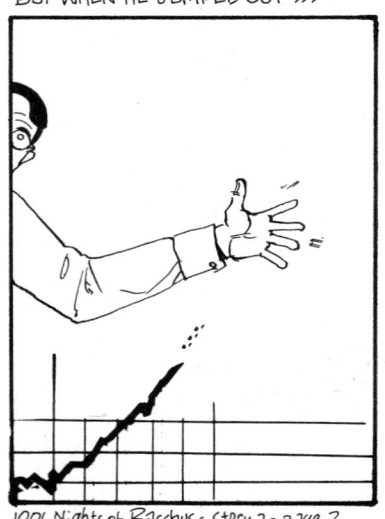

ACTUALLY, IT WASN'T MUCH OF A SURPRISE ANYHOW, BECAUSE THE DINNER WAS CHICKEN CASSEROLE.

Serving Suggestion

AND THIS *WAS* WEDNESDAY, AFTER ALL.

AS IT HAPPENS, THE THOUGHT HAD CROSSED HIS MIND THAT HE COULD SWOP DINNERS WITH THURSDAY.

BUT WHEN HE LOOKED IN THE FRIDGE HE REMEMBERED THAT THURSDAY WAS SHOPPING DAY, SO THURSDAY'S DINNER HADN'T BEEN PURCHASED YET.

IT OCCURRED TO HIM ON THE OTHER HAND THAT WEDNESDAY IS BANK DAY...

...AND THUS, SINCE HE HAD ALREADY TAKEN THE SHOPPING MONEY OUT OF THE BANK, HE COULD THEORETICALLY GO OUT AND BUY THURSDAY'S DINNER ONE DAY IN ADVANCE.

BUT THAT WOULD MEAN JUGGLING THE FIGURES IN THE HOUSEHOLD ACCOUNTING BOOK, HE ARGUED WITH HIMSELF.

BUT THE BOOK ONLY EXISTS IN HIS HEAD, HE CONCLUDED, SO HE COULD QUITE EASILY JUST SAY BUGGER THE ACCOUNTS.

BUT THE MAN WHO COULDN'T SAY BOO DIDN'T HAVE A HOPE IN HELL OF SAYING BUGGER THE ACCOUNTS.

1001 Nights of Bacchus Story 2 - page 3

THE MAN WHO COULDN'T SAY BOO EXPERIENCED AN ANNOYING HINDRANCE THAT NIGHT...

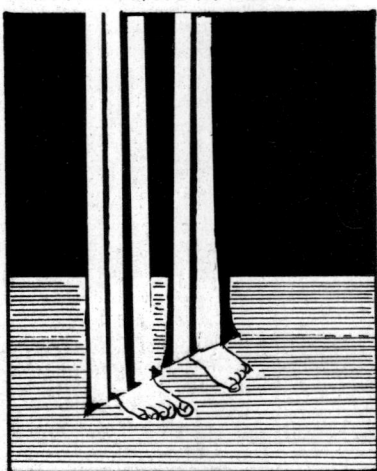
THE NEW GIRL WHO DOES THE LAUNDRY HAD IRONED HIS PYJAMAS WITH THE CREASES AT THE SIDES.

HE STAYED UP LATE AND DID THE IRONING ALL OVER AGAIN.

HE MENTALLY DISMISSED THE GIRL.

BUT HE COULDN'T. HE PHONED THE AGENCY. HE LEFT A MESSAGE ON THEIR MACHINE FOR THE GIRL TO PHONE HIM TOMORROW.

THEN HE CHANGED THE RECORDING ON HIS OWN MACHINE.

"YOU'RE FIRED!"

HE MADE A CUP OF TEA. THEN HE SAW THE FOOLISHNESS OF IT ALL.

HE ERASED THE MESSAGE TO THE GIRL FROM HIS MACHINE, THEN TRIED TO GET HIS ORIGINAL RECORDING BACK EXACTLY THE WAY IT WAS...

"Leave your message after the boop... no, hold it.. start again."

HE PHONED THE AGENCY.

"CANCEL MY EARLIER MESSAGE!"

1001 Nights of Bacchus - Story 2 - page 4

THE MAN WHO COULDN'T SAY BOO'S WIFE HAD ROLLED IN HER SLEEP. SHE WAS ON HIS SIDE OF THE BED.

HE TRIED TO SLEEP ON HERS, BUT THE TERMITES IN THE WALL KEPT HIM AWAKE.

HE ESSAYED TO EXCAVATE HER BACK TO HER OWN SIDE AND AFTER MUCH EFFORT MET WITH PARTIAL SUCCESS,

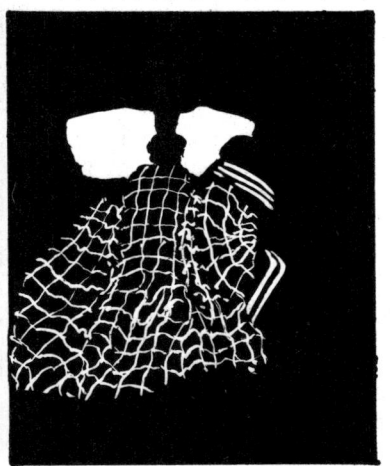

HE DREAMED THAT THE ORDERED FABRIC OF THE UNIVERSE WAS COMING APART...

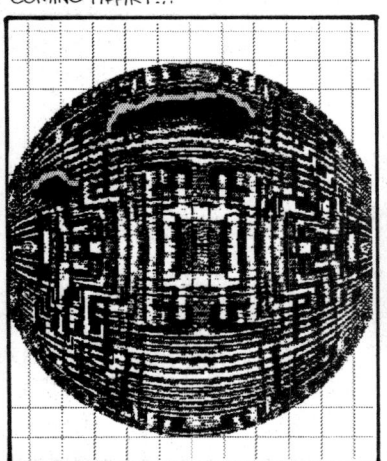

...AND THAT BUGS WERE EATING THE SYSTEM FROM THE INSIDE...

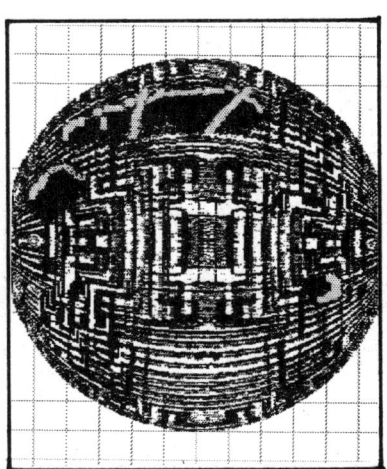

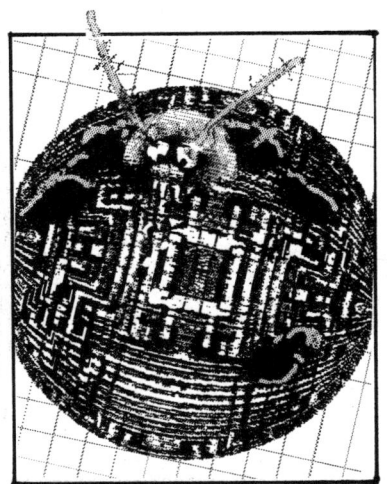

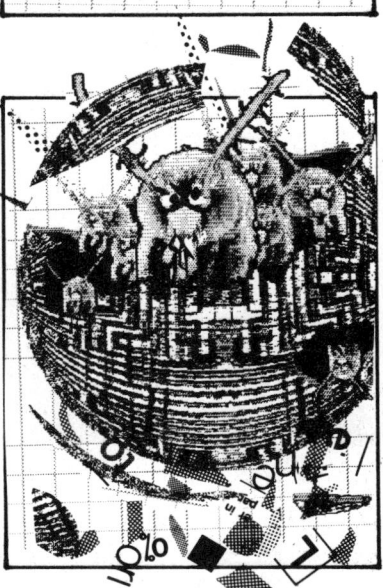

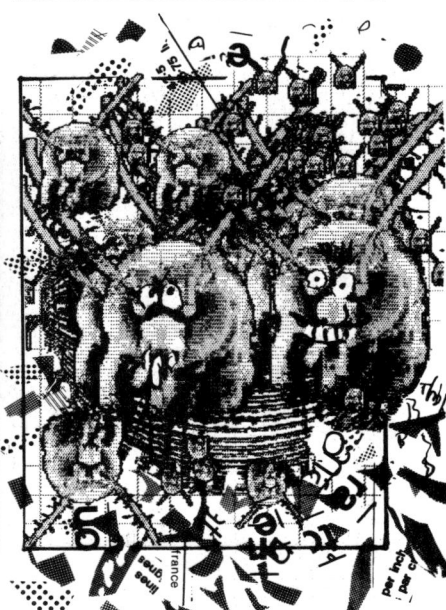

1001 Nights of Bacchus · Story 2 · page 5

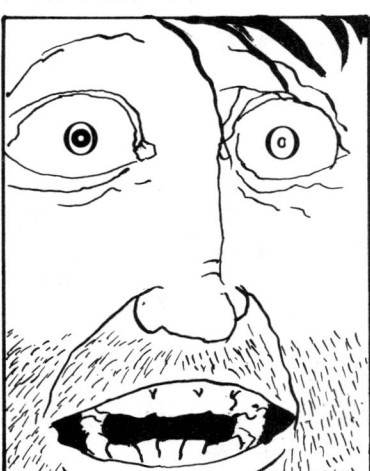

THE MAN WHO COULDN'T SAY BOO CORRECTLY SURMISED THAT THIS CATASTROPHE WOULD NOT HAVE HAPPENED HAD HE BEEN ON TIME. 	EVERY EYE WAS UPON HIM AS HE ENTERED THE OFFICE, LATE. 	EVERY EYE FOLLOWED HIM AS HE WALKED THE LENGTH OF THE OFFICE TO HIS CUBICLE. 
EVERY EYE CONDEMNED HIM FOR HIS LATENESS. 	THEY WEREN'T TO KNOW ABOUT THE BICYCLE. 	HOW COULD THEY POSSIBLY IMAGINE THE CASCADE OF CALAMITIES THAT HAD BEFALLEN HIM IN THE LAST TWELVE HOURS? 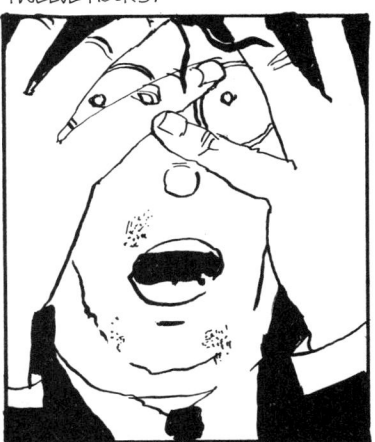
THEY DO NOT HAVE THE INSIGHT TO DIVINE THAT THE SYSTEM IS ALREADY HALF-EATEN BY BUGS. 	AND THEN HE NOTICED IT... 	ONE OF HIS PENCILS WAS MISSING. 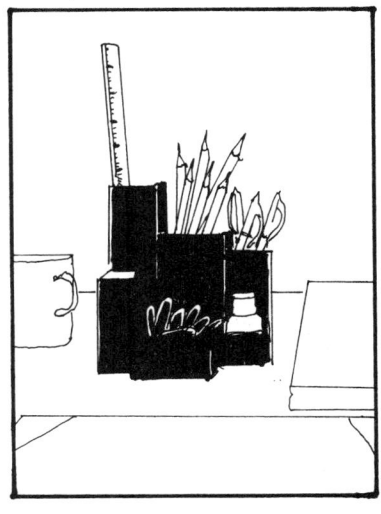

1001 Nights of Bacchus - story 2 - page 7

It was a loud night: too many noises, too many faces, too many lights. I voyaged to the bottom of too many bottles to drown it out.

Anyways, by the time my body pulled the plug on my brain, I must have been looking for the heart of the night with a white cane.

I woke up I knew not where. Something dripped and my hand felt something wet.

I was in a hole.

Correction, I was in somebody else's hole.

Suddenly things became dark. It was a total eclipse maybe, or a flying saucer about to land.

Holy Toledo! It was a coffin. I was about to be crushed brains under someone's mortal remains.

Jeez, what would these people think?

I remembered something I saw on the Late Late Show and acted as though I was a grave-digger there to help with the descent of the deceased.

I couldn't leave without looking stupid, so I stayed and watched the rest of the funeral.

No one cried. Most of the people looked bored or embarrassed, or put on that martyred expression frigid dames do when their husbands go prospecting.

The kids played tag behind the adults.

The only people who looked comfortable were the undertaker and the priest. It must have been like the fifth year in a Broadway show for them.

They were getting paid. Disgusting. Folks can't take it with them, so the vicar cuts it off. A good living, eh? Death and taxes, the two inevitabilities in life and after you're gone...

"AND THE DEATH TAXES SHALL INHERIT THE EARTH. AMEN."

After the government, the lawyers, the undertaker, and the clergy had taken their bite out of his mortal remains, I'd be surprised if there was anything left for the worms.

That's when I felt this itching sensation in the side of my head... there was something moist in it...

...A worm!

I chucked my cookies and fell down on the grave, overcome by the reek and nausea.

Then the strangest thing occurred.

"Bobok."
"Bobok."

1001 Nights of Bacchus · story 3 · page 3

I, the avengin' angel o' the Lord, had heaps o' trouble gettin' me wings inside the sports jacket. 	None o' us like the Avengin', but the chief found a speck o' dust on Mike's sword an' Mike got the night shift. 	Gabe got caught wi' his trumpet in hock, an' now Gabe's blowin' the bellows down below.
That left me, the Angel Seamus, as the only available boy for the job. 	Thank Jayzus it was a typical mornin'. 	Someone forgot Lot's wife. 
Someone said *fool* to his brother. 	Someone suffered a witch to live. 	'Twas the afternoon when the bother would start, if only I did but know. 

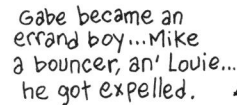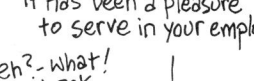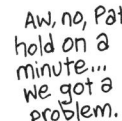

Time's wearin' on, an' the poor body's lyin' there in the sun.

I starts in tellin' him to go to Hell but I pulls meself up short just in time. No profit in bein' facetious.

But it sounds all hopeless. I'll just have to come clean.

1001 Nights of Bacchus- story W4 page 7

me next recourse is to attempt a cover-up.

"Louie, ye could just let the soul go and no one would be any the wiser."

I considers some desperate plea-bargaining:

"They can't get me for bein' thou-a-wine-bibber since I was drinkin' the black stuff."

I throws meself upon the tender mercies o' the court.

"Pete, I dropped meself in the poo."

But Louie's carryin' a heavy grudge these days. His demands exceed the authority o' this poor boy to give.

"but you've already got New York."

"They can't get me for bein' a soul poacher... At best I'm a receiver after the fact."

"don't tell me... Apocryphal."

"yup."

MA QUEST — TO GO TE THE LAIRD O THE SEV7N CEDARS an CUtt DOON THE CEDAR O MA HEARTS DESIRE

WE TAK IT OFF THE ELEVEN DEMONS

A BRING 5o tae HELP

LADS WI NEETHER WIVES NOR MOTHERS te SUPPORT

IT WAS THEM WHO HEFTED the TIMBER AFF

WE WERE LYIN PISHED WHEN ONKY DOO TRIED TE WAKE ME BEFOR the HooWooWA COME

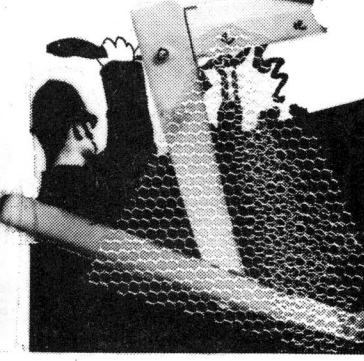

BUT THEN ONKY DOO SED HE LOST The DALGLEESH JERSEY

an HE HAS TO GO DOON TE the NETHER World TE GET IT BACK

SO A GI HIM AW THE ADVICE A CAN THINK O SHITE A WISH A WAS DED

WHAT YA DESERVE ta die!

1001 Nights of Bacchus · story 5 · page 3

AN A SAY, THIS WHEN YE GO BAK te the PUB ye do these things exactly As A tell ye

ONE YE WOK IN LIKE YE bEEn THERE EVERY dAy O yuRe LIfe

an YE DONT ASk FOR HEAVY YE DRink THE ENGLISH PISH

WELL ONKY DOO gOES DOON THERE AN FORGETS aw A TOLD HIM

How many Englishmen does it take tae change a lightbulb?

Two. one te hold the ladder an the other te kiss ma arse.

ENDS UP IN A FIX

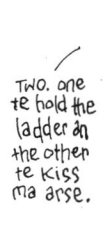

HE GETS TRAPPED BY the BEINS O the NETHERWORLD

AN THEN AW GET SUCK IN W THEIR CHIBS

AN LAtER HE FELL OVER DED IN MA ARMS

A SHOULDA GONE WI The brave WEE FULE A LET HIM DOON A MIGHT AS WELL A WIELDED THE KNIFE ma SEL

1001 Nights of Bacchus - Story 5 - page 4

WHAT AM A SUPPOSED TE DO STUCK ON THIS GOD FORSAKEN TURF

TE HAVE THE HANGOVER AN PAY FOR IT TOO THERES THE RUB O THE JOCKSTRAP THAT FITS TOO CLOSE

A LOOKED INTE THE FOUNTIN O TRAFALGAR SQUARE AN SAW AW THE FLOATIN BODYS

THAT COULD BE ME

THEN A NOTIS SOMETHIN ELS THER WURNT ANY WUMMIN

THEN A SAW A SACRED BEACON BECKONIN TE ME FRAE THE TOPE O A DOUBLE DECKER BUS

ALL AT ONCE A THOT THATS WERRA OTTA BE

SO THATS WHY AM HERE

IF THIS IS THE END O THE WORLD WITS THE FINAL SCORE

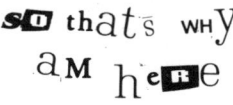

1001 Nights of Bacchus - story 5 - page 5

This year we win
Next year the English
Tek it back Come
the end o the world
who keeps it

Who gets the last
sip o the shampein
an wher dus
it go

A mean for those
o us who pay by
tick wits the final
tally

Is there any chance
at aw o us gettin
any more credit

Look what do you want
luv I serve drinks til
closing time and what
happens after that aint
none of my business

You can have your ale
bitter or sweet luv
you can try and chat
me up or you can
pretend youre impress
ing me by playing
the smoothie

One things certain luv
you came in with the
draught when the pub
was open and like the
beer youre drinking
youll go out with it
when the bar closes

Its like luv innit luv
youre never really
certain are you you get
a nervous feeling like
and feel awkward and
stupid whenever youre
near the bastard

And make a fool of
yourself doing whatever
he wants and even though
you think youre happy
you wonder if you
really are

1001 Nights ot Bacchus story 5 page 6

i mean you dont know what luv is do you let me serve this other chap best wasn't it

its what everybody talks About luv and what people say when you know when they want to make luv

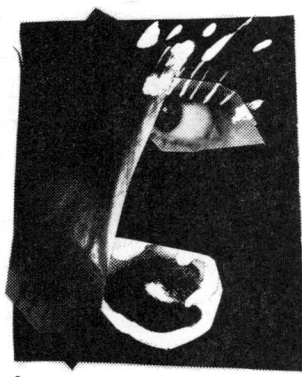

But does Anyone ever really experience it or is it like God a good idea that might not even exist

but that aunt the problem the problem is that once you start questioning it it doesnt work another port and lemon coming up

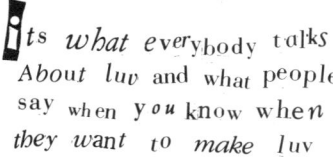

i mean it's like looking for the perfect fella youre never satisFied Because you think That Just around the corner there might be a better One

The whole point luv is to build up the slate while youre alive so you can have a good time when youre dead BY not paying It

eh

Arent you listening whoever survives the Party has to clean up

A tOOk hER aDvicE an LefT witHoot PAyiN

1001 Nights of Bacchus story 5 page 7

RUBBING GENIE THE WRONG WAY

Eddie Campbell with Marcus Moore 5-96

"DO WHAT, JOHN?"

"I THINK YOU'LL FIND HE WANTS A PINT OF HANCOCK'S, HECTOR."

"WELL HASN'T HE GOT A BLOODY TONGUE IN 'IS 'EAD.?"

"MAYBE NOT. HE IS DRESSED AS A MIME AFTER ALL."

"WELL HOW THE HELL DID YOU KNOW WHAT HE WANTED?"

"IT WAS THE GESTURES. CHARADES, WEREN'T IT. HE PULLED THAT SOUR FACE; HE WANTED A BITTER, SEE?"

1001 Nights of Bacchus - story 6 - page 1

Sagittarius
Someone close to you will go on a long journey. Avoid cheese.

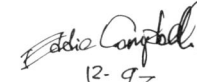

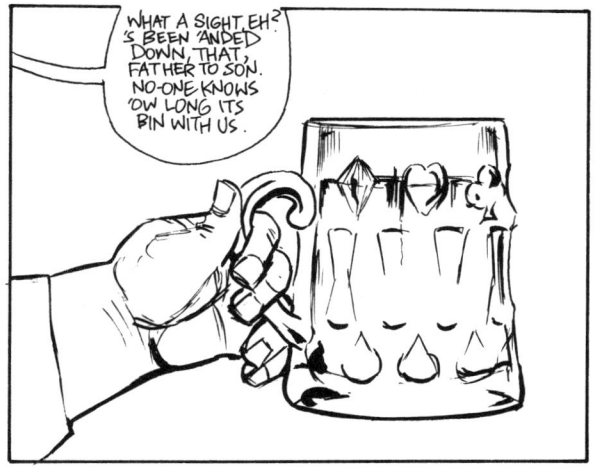

I call upon all who do imbibe
   to hear this tale I tell.
     I sing of a cursed ale that's brewed
        midst brimstone down in Hell.
    Through all of time
       this beer has sought
          out those who would excel.
    It's touched the lips
       of life's great men,
          and great no more,
             they fell.

To times anew from days of old,
  passed down from son to dad.
  So hear the advice I give to you,
    beware the beer that's bad.

Poor Hitler he's tucked up,
in his bunker there in cosy Berlin.
It's '45, he's still alive,
this war he still could win.
With fav'rite stein
he toasts his luck,
a gift from Himmler to him.
But the door's not locked,
his luger's not cocked
and look who now creeps in.

So sup ye not the cursed ale,
don't tap that cask, you'd be mad,
But hear the advice I give to you,
beware the beer that's bad.

Now Eliot Ness, was not a man
you'd sway too easily.
The sobrest of sorts
with noblest thoughts,
tee-totaller was he.
When busting breweries
one late night his iron will
did flee.
"Aw one won't hurt" he thought, alas;
the rest is history.

So if you lose your way and mourn
the fun you have not had,
Please hear the advice I give to you,
beware the beer that's bad.

• • •

In his last, liquor-sodden years, Eliot Ness entered a spiral of decline. In 1948 he returned to the Diebold Safe Company, commuting forty miles from his rented home in Cleveland to Canton. However, he spent more time on the road, drinking, than he did in his office. Each day he would stop in Kent, Ohio, for more than a few drinks. While drifting through...

In all of drinking history
the examples are so vast,
But three's enough for us tonight
my song it soon shall pass.
So spare a thought for those sad bas
tards as you lift your glass,
Then down your beer and give a cheer
and hope it's not your last.

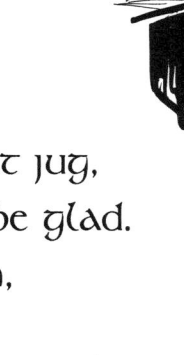

Pick up that tumbler, grab that jug,
throw back that grain and be glad.
Of the advice I have given,
you soon may be ridden,
drink up lest your ale turn bad.

What does it all mean?' asked the Caliph

1001 Nights of Bacchus · story 9 · page 1

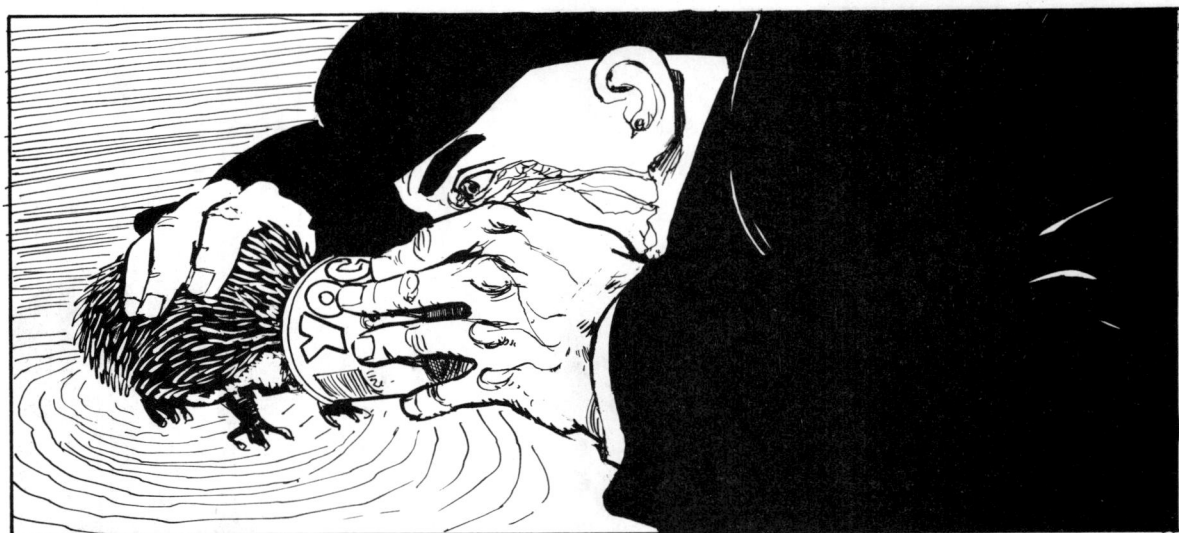

Have as many eyes as you like.

Eddie Campbell
6 • 98
Daren (The Look) White

"IF YOU ARE ALL SITTING COMFORTABLY, THEN I SHALL BEGIN..."

"I WAS WONDERING WHEN YOU WERE GOING TO DO THE HONOURS. YOU'VE BEEN SITTING THERE NIGHT AFTER NIGHT GETTING EVERYBODY ELSE TO TELL THE STORIES."

"AND IT WILL BE WORTH THE WAIT, MY OLD SON. YOU JUST LISTEN..."

1001 Nights of Bacchus - story 10 - page 1

So me and Childsie are having a quiet beer when we notice a group of kids who were about four years below us at school

Most of them are only just eighteen and they seem to be celebrating the end of their exams or something

I make eye contact with one of the girls and suddenly I realise that it's the girl that Childsie set alight about five years earlier

Now, I don't mean that she fell in love with him or anything - he actually set her on fire

see we were sitting on the bus home from school and he had this box of matches which he was gormlessly flicking down the aisle.

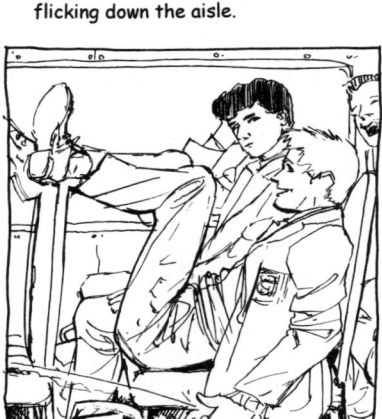

now I kept telling him to put the fucking matches away because sooner or later someone was going to get hurt and the chances were it would be me

but no, he knew better. The next thing, one of the matches landed on this girl's arm

and she was wearing some sort of poly-vinyl plastic shit trendy new jacket and like woosh the whole fucking sleeve went up

now at this point Childsie started to panic and luckily managed to smother the flames before the girl got hurt.

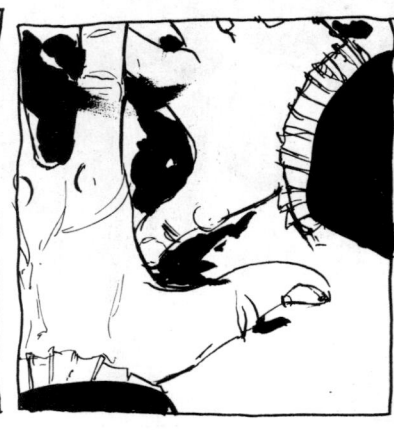

crisis over except the girls got this fucking great big whole in the sleeve of her poly-vinyl plastic shit trendy new jacket

well at this point me and Dilkes were starting to see the funny side of things and I was saying "there's no need to flare up!" and he was saying "she's a hot one!"

and Childsie was just sitting there fucking relieved that no one was scarred for life or anything

The girl was probably suffering from mild shock and she had a fucking great big hole in the sleeve of her new poly-vinyl plastic shit trendy new jacket

and the whole bus was giggling and she turned to me as her eyes started to fill up and she gave me the look.

Well suddenly I didn't feel like laughing anymore. I mean the poor cow was sitting there minding her own business, probably wondering what was for tea that night

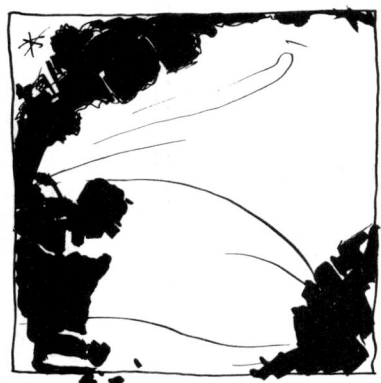

and worrying about getting her chemistry homework done when suddenly some prick sets her on fire.

A flash of de ja vu and I'm back in junior school. Nicola Stapleton, who wasn't the most popular girl in class,

has just brought in her new Kermit the frog

1001 Nights of Bacchus - Story 10 page 3

Now the muppets haven't been around too long at that point and so bringing Kermit into school was a bit of a coo.

This meant that Nicola was suddenly being invited to play with the in-crowd who normally relegated her to the same collection of excommunicated nobodies as

Gina Nash, who committed the most grievous of mortal sins by becoming the first girl in the class to menstruate.

Anyway, Nicola was laughing and smiling and immersing herself in what may well have been her only fifteen minutes of fame when Kermit's arm came clean off.

As she stared in horror at Kermit's mutilated form her somewhat brief encounter with fame came to an abrupt end

and worse, the spiteful bitches from the in crowd were no longer laughing with her but at her and what the fuck was her mum going to say

when she learned that not only had Kermit been taken to school but was also now crippled. Well, her eyes filled up and she too gave me the look.

Now, I'm back in the pub, And the girl's giving me a different look which says I know you

and I remember that you had something to do with one of the most humiliating and hurtful days in my life, but I'm over that now and I'm safe

and confident because I'm with my friends   and I've finished my exams and I'll probably get really good grades and   get a good job with a future.

and they obviously think he's a sad sap as well because nobody will move up so that he can sit down

because she's with her cool college friend and he doesn't belong to this part of her life.

and then suddenly her boyfriend appears and fucking hell it's Justin Potter, who's some sad sap that I went to scouts with.

and she's feeling really embarrassed because although he's her boyfriend and she probably does have some genuine affection for him

So the poor sap's standing there in his dreadful suit with his bottom lip hanging down the way it always does

Well Potter's wearing some fucking dreadful suit and he's older than the others

she sure as shit doesn't want him hanging around at this precise moment in time

and like no one is going to move up so that he can sit down

Potter does the decent thing and buys a round of drinks.

They're fucking students, after all, and as such can only drink three pints before throwing up, besides which none of them have got any money

Having returned from the bar Potter gives up the ghost and contents himself with standing behind his girlfriend

1001 Nights of Bacchus - story 10 - page 6

Well, the least cool of the college friends obviously cracks with guilt and moves up a few inches so that Potter can get at least one cheek on the sofa

and so having already chocked up for a round of drinks for a bunch of wankers that he doesn't even like, Potter must now buy himself another beer

but, wait for it, in a defiant bid to stake his claim against any of the college wankers making a move on his bird, he casually drapes his hand over her shoulder

However, Potter's luck runs dry because he's drinking with a bunch of students who all seem somewhat reticent towards buying him a drink back.

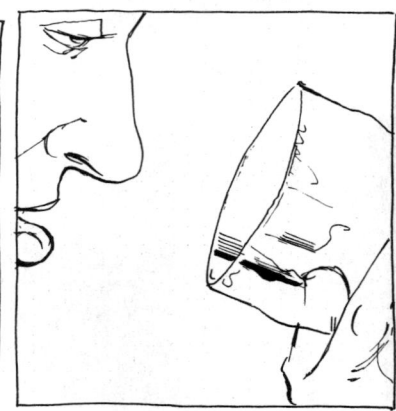

so he pops up to the bar and the least cool of the college crowd, having done his bit for charity and fully exorcised his guilt, reclaims Potters cheek space.

Well, the girl cringes with embarrassment and as her eyes begin to fill she gives me the look.

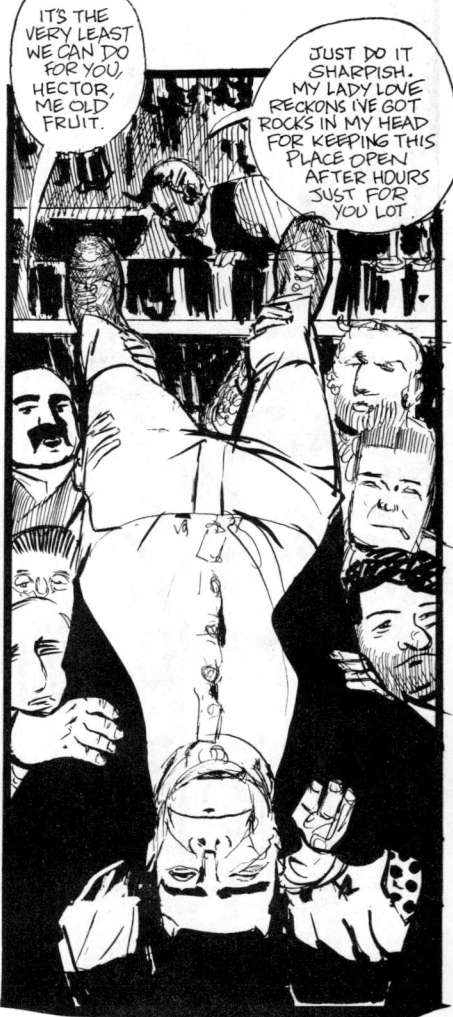

DO YOU BELIEVE IN GHOSTS?
I NEVER USED TO. MAN OF SCIENCE, ME. MORE OF A SCULLY THAN A MULDER. O-LEVELS IN RATIONAL BEHAVIOUR

BUT THAT WAS BEFORE I SAW THE BED

YOU SEE, I'M A CHIROPODIST, SO I GOT THE FACTS FIRST HAND. AND BEFORE YOU SAY IT, NO I'M NOT SOME KIND OF FOOT WEIRDO LIKE FERGIE.

I REALLY WANTED TO BE A GYNAECOLOGIST BUT I DIDN'T GET GOOD ENOUGH GRADES. DIDN'T KNOW ME BITS FROM ME PIECES, AS IT WERE.

ANYWAY, I'M GETTING OFF THE TRACK.

I'M ON NIGHTS AT THE GENERAL HOSPITAL AND I'M SUPPOSED TO SERVICE THE INTENSIVE CARES.

WELL I'D DONE A CLEAN AND GLEAN ON THAT NICE MR. NEWBY IN BED SEVEN AND WAS ABOUT TO GET ME HEAD DOWN FOR AN HOUR.

WHEN ALL HELL BROKE LOOSE

DOCTORS FLAPPED, NURSES COLLAPSED. AND THAT NICE MR. NEWBY WAS STONE COLD DEAD

The 1001 Nights of Bacchus - story 12 - page 3

A FEW DAYS PASSED AND THINGS RETURNED TO NORMAL. NO MORE MR. NEWBY, BUT THIS WAS A HOSPITAL AFTER ALL.

THESE THINGS HAPPEN.

THEN ANOTHER ONE COUGHED, SAME TIME OF NIGHT AND IN THE SAME BED.

I COULDN'T BELIEVE IT.

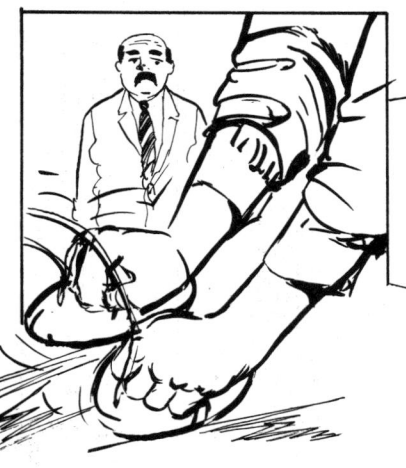

WORSE, OVER THE NEXT FEW WEEKS WE LOST ANOTHER THREE. I MEAN, IT DIDN'T LOOK GOOD, DID IT?

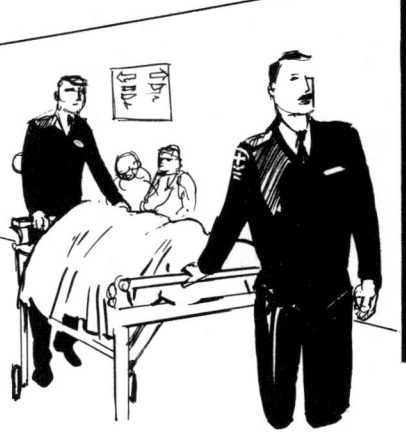

IF THE PATIENTS WERE GONNA DIE ANYWAY THEY MIGHT AS WELL HAVE STAYED HOME.

WELL THE MEN IN SUITS FROM THE FIFTH FLOOR OBVIOUSLY PANICKED, BECAUSE IT SEEMED LIKE HALF THE BLEEDING STAFF WERE SUSPENDED.

WHICH OF COURSE BROUGHT THE UNIONS INTO IT.

AND NEXT THING WE WERE STARING DOWN BOTH BARRELS OF AN ALL OUT STRIKE

OF COURSE NOBODY ASKED ME. I COULD HAVE TOLD THEM.
 IT WASN'T THE STAFF IT WAS THE BLOODY BED.

IT WAS HAUNTED.

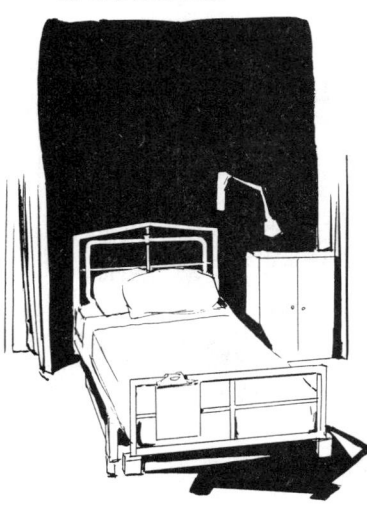

WELL THE NURSES ENDED UP WALKING OUT

AND THEN AMBULANCE DRIVERS STARTED WORKING TO RULE.

AND THE NATIONAL HEALTH BROUGHT IN THIS HIGH POWERED YANK SPECIALIST SORT IT ALL OUT.

THE OUTCOME OF THE WHOLE THING WAS THAT THREE OF THE SUITS GOT SIDEWAYS SHUFFLES

THE NEWSPAPERS FOUND OUT THAT TWO OF THE NURSES DID A BIT OF STRIPPING ON THE SIDE

AND NOBODY DID ANYTHING ABOUT THE BED. SO IT CAME AS NO SURPRISE TWO WEEKS LATER WHEN ANOTHER ONE DROPPED DEAD.

WHICH AGAIN WENT DOWN LIKE A SACK OF SHIT WITH THE MEN IN SUITS AND STARTED A WITCH HUNT FOR ANOTHER LIKELY SCAPE GOAT.

1001 Nights of Bacchus story 12 · page 5

WELL BELIEVE IT OR NOT SOME JUMPED UP SUIT GOES AND FORMS A CORRELATION BETWEEN THE DEATHS AND MY PEDICURES.

AND SUDDENLY EVERYTHING'S MY FUCKING FAULT. SO I'M OUT ON MY EAR FACING AN INVOLUNTARY CHANGE OF CAREER PATH. NO SYMPATHETIC UNION IS THREATENING TO DO ONE ON MY BEHALF

AND THE DEMONIC BED IS STILL HAPPILY SUCKING THE LIFE FORCE OUT OF ANY POOR SAP WHO HAS THE MISFORTUNE TO BECOME A RESIDENT OF THE INTENSIVE CARE CORNER UNIT.

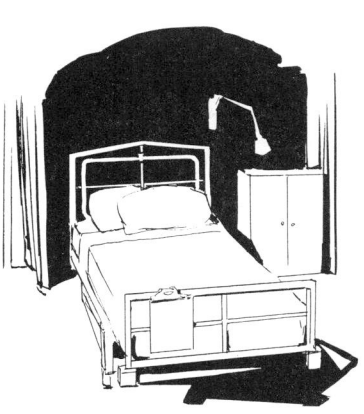

I'M TELLING YOU THERE AIN'T NO JUSTICE ANY MORE

AND WHEN IT COMES TO GHOSTS, WELL I'M WITH THE MONKEES.

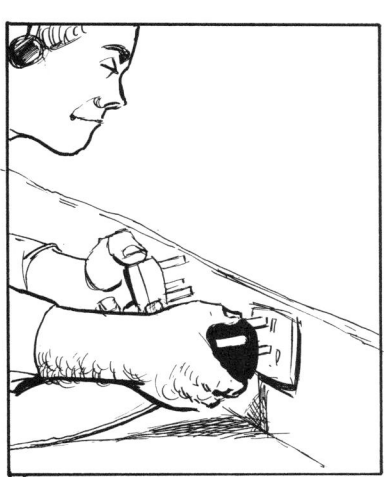

LIKE I SAID, I'M A BELIEVER.

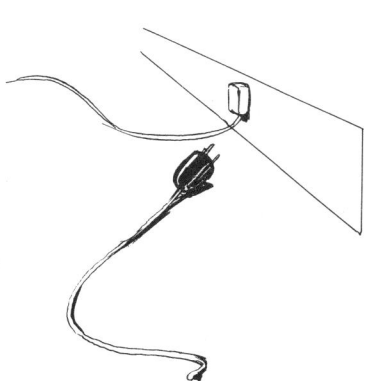

1001 Nights of Bacchus - story 12 - page 6.

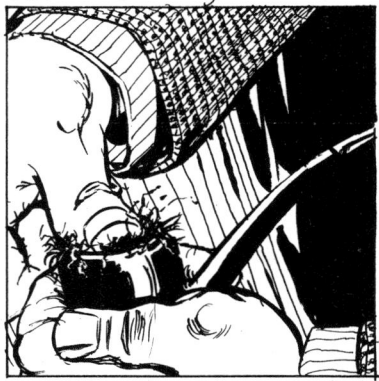

He massaged the point on his nose where his glasses had been.

"We... a man, and a woman, in a loving relationship, who are married..."

Mr. Pownall had charge of his train of thought. And the boys were so glad they almost waved it goodbye as they sensed it chugging out of the station. Each one of them was truly thankful that the powwow was underway.

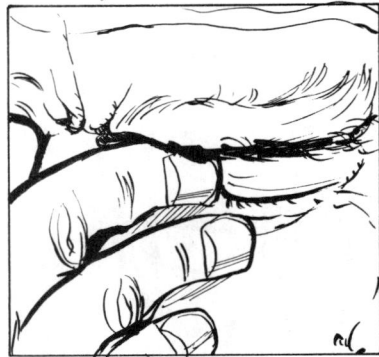

There was always a degree of fiddling around as if he was blowing fluff off a gramophone needle or something but pretty soon the record was in place and the gentle rise and fall of his voice meant he'd got further away from the point.

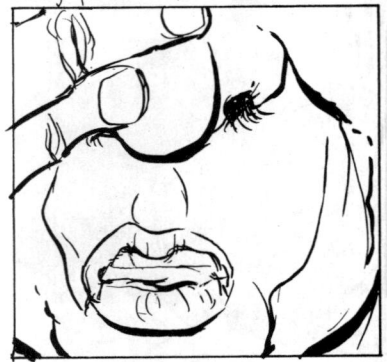

Now. Stood next to Michael Dalton was Andrew Cameron and for his birthday he'd been given a Timex watch which frogmen wore at a depth of fifty feet. Or so he said.

It had a large blue face and when it caught the sun beating in through the window it cast a silvery blue disc upon the ceiling. He started playing with the effect just to relieve the boredom at first.

But then with careful guidance he found that he could land the double circle on old Powlie's lapels. Because Michael Dalton's gaze had never been frozen on any one object he was first to notice that the Mysterons were on the move.

He saw the agitation of the blue monarch shift from Powlie's shoulder to his tie and followed its palsied caresses of his cheek and chin before it settled on his eyes like a jittering racoon mask.

Mr. Pownall was rubbing his short-sighted eyes not for any irritation caused by the blue light but because he was into a delicate area. He'd taken on a tough brief

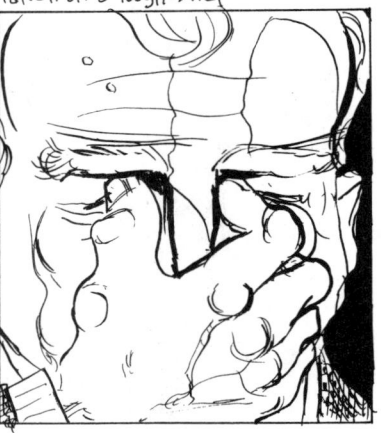

He had to train a soft light onto human sexuality in order to bring a welder's lamp to the baseness of pornography. He had the uncomfortable feeling he was doing something of a striptease himself.

Human Qualities - page 3

He had to show enough of his argument using simple intellectual gestures but not get clumsy and start showing too much. Where was he? Yes...

So we must never lose sight of that sensitivity to the relationship between a man and a woman. Pictures of men and women for entertainment... is a hundred miles away from what I'm talking about.

The two other boys were as eager as Dalton to see the blue spot get back onto Powie's nose again. It seemed to have a personality all of its own. and there was an exhilarating cheekiness in the way it nibbled his ears and then tried to disappear up his nose.
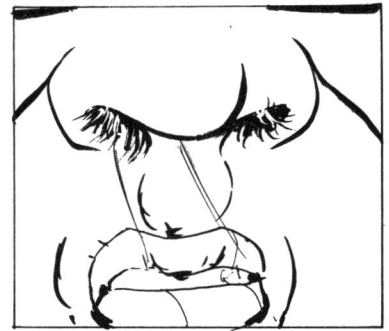

Less and less now did it shyly settle on the wall behind in wait. Now it had a delightful recklessness. All about the room it went; the ceiling, Powie's hair; it was as if it was colouring his face in. The slapstick of the bright butterfly was as completely compelling as —

There's nothing funny about this, Dalton! Nothing at all! I hope I've made myself perfectly clear.

Clear as mud as he was well aware.

Now if I catch any one of you with this kind of material again, you'll be expelled. D'you understand me?

Go back to class. All of you.

After they'd shambled out, Mr. Pownall lit up his pipe before looking through the magazines again.

END.

THE TRAGIC HISTORY OF THE CASTLE AND FROG IS FULLY TOLD IN *KING BACCHUS* on sale from the proprietors.